WELCOME TO OLIVER'S
ADVENTURE

Oliver is a lovable Maltipoo with a big heart and an even bigger imagination. When he's not chasing tennis balls or taking cozy naps, Oliver loves teaching kids new things especially their ABCs! Inspired by his own adventures around the neighborhood (and a few snack breaks in between), Oliver decided to write this book to make learning the alphabet fun for everyone. With his wagging tail and a head full of ideas, Oliver hopes to help kids everywhere fall in love with letters, words, and storytelling.

DEDICATION

For Nancy, who taught us that ice cream is a meal

Oliver's ABCs

ISBN: 979-8-9932198-2-0
ISBN: 979-8-9932198-3-7

Published by Boundless Book Publishers

www.boundlessbookpublishers.com

A is for Apple

B is for Ball

C is for Cat

D is for Dragon

E is for Elephant

F is for Fish

G is for Guitar

H is for Hat

I is for Ice Cream

J is for Jump

K is for Kite

L is for Lion

M is for Mail

N is for Nap

O is for Orange

P is for Paint

Q is for Queen

R is for Rocket

S is for Star

T is for Towel

U is for Umbrella

V is for violin

W is for Watermelon

X is for X-ray

Y is for Yarn

Z is for Zebra

TRACING THE LETTERS!

A B C D E

F G H I J

K L M N O

P Q R S T

U V W X

Y Z

COLORING THE LETTERS!

A B C D E

F G H I J

K L M N O

P Q R S T

U V W X

Y Z

www.ingramcontent.com/pod-product-compliance
Lightning Source LLC
Chambersburg PA
CBHW042135120726
47911CB00022B/94